Might & Glory

Μήπως και Δόξα

Ronald J. McNutt

Might
&
Glory
Μήπως και Δόξα

Written by:

Ronald J. McNutt, ©2014

ISBN: 978-0-9892843-3-2

Table of Contents

My son, do not follow me into battle. Do not follow me into that long dark night of the soul where the light does not shine. Here there is no warmth. There is no friend. Only sword and shield in the cold night alone.

Carry on my son. Carry on as best you may. Live your life and make love to your woman. Fight if you must but know this, there is no glory in war. Only death and blood in butchery. There is no honor in the blood of your friend as it sprays your face and rains down your armor.

Remember this my son, the ones you kill are your brothers, your fathers, your sons. Their faces will haunt your dreams. Their cold, lifeless spirits will gather 'round you in the night and whisper "come my brother, my father, my son. Join us in the land of the dead."

Take up your arms my son, if you must. Lift your sword and raise the battle cry but remember, he lives by the sword shall die by the sword.

So fight on my son. Pour out your strength until your enemies fall at your feet and your banner waves over the battlefield. But be not mistaken, this is not glory.

The glory goes to the one who does not fall back or retreat. The one who looks upon his numberless enemies and stands his ground.

Do not fear their faces. Do not fear their spears or glittering armor. Remember that they too tremble even as they advance.

So face your enemy with boldness. My son, a calm mind, a peaceful heart, and a steady hand - this is a more grievous weapon than the edge of the sharpest sword and gives you the advantage over your adversary.

Be strong. Be courageous. And if you fall, rise and rise again until your hand is stronger than he who is against it. There is but one difference between the hero and the defeated: the hero will always rise again.

Remember these words my son, and do not forget them. Every generation has its war. Triumph then, and may your days be clothed in glory.

*   *   *

He folded the letter carefully and slid it into the folds of the infants blankets. He looked down at child, the son of his brother. He looked down for long time, his weather-beaten face hiding the remorse behind.

"Until we meet again child" he said softly. He turned, slung his rounded shield upon his back, and begin the long journey home.

Athens was very far away.

Two nations, both alike in might and stature, rose to the height of power long ago. For many ages, their borders and influence expanded across Mediterranea unchecked by any rival save only mighty Egypt. To the north, Athens grew and spread across the Greek Isles. To the west, Atlantia arose and sought to conquer the sea.

In time, as their borders expanded, conflict began; each one claiming the rights of the sea and the trade routes. Finally, Atlantia, full of pride in malice, launched an assault upon Athens. A great sea battle ensued, and as the last Atlantian ship sunk off the Athenian shore, the victory descended upon the Greeks.

It took many years and countless lives of brave men, but in time the Athenians fought their way to the very shore of the Atlantian capital.

He knelt down and opened his hand. Placing it gently onto the soil, he closed his eyes. He felt the mass of the Earth sway beneath the sun and in the depths of his spirit he felt the gears of the world turning. But then there were something else. Somewhere in the depths of the Earth something stirred. Like a great dragon rising, it sent a tremor through the land. He felt it now, just on the edge of his conscious mind. A whisper. A ghost. A phantom of dark foreboding.

With staff in hand, he stood and looked toward the towering mountain. It's lofty summit was shrouded in clouds. For a long time he considered the matter, for surely great and terrible events were close at hand.

The mountain had awoken.

From where he stood, he could see both the mountain and the sparkling city of Atlantia down below. From his home upon the high plain, the city looked peaceful. A pearl rising from the ocean glittering in the sun. It's lofty walls and spires were unassailable and its mighty influence reached across the whole of Oceana and Mediterranea. This was the city of Kings. Or so it was, long ago.

For many years, the old man watched as ruler after ruler, King after King chose ever darkening paths until the whole of his subjects descended with him. Where there was once reason and wisdom there was now superstition and evil witchcraft. Ever seeking riches and immortality, the Kings of Atlantia fell to ruin and depravity, spending its greatness on wine and lustful indulgence.

The land itself had given warnings against this evil. The crops had begun to fail. The fish in the bay were no more. The birds themselves, once so magnificent in their colors and numbers, perched no more on the island of Atlantia. And now, it seemed the Earth herself had had enough.

Lionisius looked on with sadness and despair.

iV

"We should take the city tonight."

"Peace, Patrus. It was not rashness that has brought us this close to victory."

"No, not rashness my brother Helio's, but boldness. The victory goes to the strong and to the brave. And who is stronger or braver than the Athenians? The gods favor us and our cause. And even if they did not, who could stand against mighty Aerocles, Althion, and the noble company gathered here?"

"Peace my brothers, peace" spoke old Quintus. "It has not been only the boldness of brave Patrus, nor the patience of steady Helio's that have pleased the gods and beaten back the Atlantian's. There is a time for boldness and there is a time for patience, both of which are proven right or wrong by the edge of the warrior sword. Consider then, my King's and fellow nobles, the hearts of the men whose spears and swords will determine this battle.

"Over the long years of continuous fighting our numbers have dwindled, and so victory through overwhelming force is no longer possible. Consider also the height and strength of the Atlantian walls. It will be no easy feat to breached their gates."

"What would you have us do then?" asked Patrus. "Starve them out? Lay siege to their city for another seven years?"

"Wisdom, noble Patrus, would have us inspire the hearts of the men before the final blow. Encourage them and capture their hearts. In doing so, no strength of arms or city wall will be unassailable."

"How do you propose we accomplish such a thing?" Asked Helios.

"Ask yourselves, who do the men follow when the fighting is fiercest, when the odds are against them? Is it not the hero Aerocles? Make him your captain and you will have your victory."

At this several nobles grumbled, yet Patrus was first to speak.

"Wise Quintus, your councils have brought about many victories as well as your skill with your own sword. Yet to make a commoner a captain sounds more like madness. Hero though Aerocles may be, and who could stand before him in his fury and live, but it would offend the gods to bestow upon him a rank amongst our own. For only the gods can determine who is worthy to be called noble."

"Is it the gods or your own pride you are worried about offending?" spoke Helios.

"I'll not be subject to a commoner" spoke Patrus sharply.

And so the argument continued long into the early hours of morning.

Aerocles, cloaked in hooded from the cold night, sat along the shore of Atlantia looking out toward the sea. Dawn was approaching. It was still dark in the early twilight. He had not seen home for seven years, and he thought of it now.

"Brother," came a soft voice from behind. "I am sorry for your loss."

"Come Althion, your presence is always a comfort" replied Aerocles. The day before, word had finally reached him that his uncle had fallen at the hands of the Atlantian's on a distant battlefield.

"I am now alone" he said, still looking toward the brightening sky. "I am all that remains of my family."

After a long silence Althion spoke.

"Perhaps it is a cold comfort, but I and the men who have followed you throughout this war are still your brothers. When it is over, your name will not be forgotten."

"A cold comfort it is" replied Aerocles. "But a comfort nonetheless." Then he continued, "I will mourn for three days. By evening of the fourth day, I will see the gates of Atlantia fall and the blood of every Atlantian flow through the streets of their burning city. Then, all will know Aerocles, son of Perocles, would not go quietly into the night."

VI

"But you are royal advisor to the King, surely he will listen to you!"

"My dear Lydia," Lionisius looked at his daughter and loved her. "The King will not hear me. Too many times I have counseled him to make peace with the Greeks that he would not have it. His own pride will be the fall of Atlantia. Whatever goodness was left was poured out on the battlefield as our brave men died for his arrogance."

"There is still goodness left in you, father" said Lydia gently, placing a hand on his weathered face.

"And in you my daughter" he said. "Yet even if Atlantia were to hold off the Greeks indefinitely, I fear the end is still upon us."

"The mountain?" she said.

"Yes, God himself has spoken against the evil that Atlantia has become. If we are to survive the coming wrath, we must leave this place."

"But where shall we go? Atlantia is all I have ever known."

"Tomorrow, during the battle, I will escape to the sea. There is a small harbor still unfounded by the Athenians there I will ready a ship. When all is in order, I will come for you. Look for me on the evening of the third day."

VII

That morning, the army of the Greeks and those of Atlantia assembled for battle. Both sides were weary of war, yet the end was near and fire burned in their hearts.

The bronze armor of the Athenians sparkled in the rising sun as they marched from their camp by the sea. So great was their numbers that to the watchmen upon the Atlantian towers they looked like a river of bronze glittering in the sunlight.

The Atlantian gates opened and their own soldiers, brave and heroic in their own armor, issued forth in silver breastplates, grieves, vambraces, and shields. They were polished to a high shine to mirror the sun and perhaps give them the advantage. They assembled themselves upon the field in front of the wall and awaited the Athenian charge.

Patrus, ever eager for battle, led the Athenians in centerfield. To his left, Helios directed the northern flank. To his right, wise Quintus directed the troops to the South.

As they advanced however, the Athenian troops soon realized that Aerocles, son of Perocles, was not among them. This caused some alarm for Aerocles was a great warrior and had rescued many Greeks from the edge of the sword. The Atlantian's too feared his blade, for he had cast many of their sons down into the dust. Althion, seeing the despair in their eyes, began to speak.

"Do not despair my brothers," he said loudly. "Aerocles has not abandon you. He will return. But for today, I, Althion, will be your champion. Rally to me, and I will lead you in victory!"

At this the brave soldiers around him lifted up a mighty war cry.

The Atlantians, hearing their shouts, trembled in their armor thinking it was Aerocles coming in great fury.

Without ceremony or invitation the battle began. Sounds of war rang out with a resounding roar as spear and shield clashed together. Deafening were the cries of men as many a brave warrior fell to the dust and were no more.

In the fray, Althion raised his sword against noble Alexius, famed Prince of Atlantia, and their fighting caused much excitement among the men. In the end, Alexius fell heavily at the feet of Althion, his armor ringing loudly about him as his face fell to the dirt.

Seeing their brave Prince fall to the ground, the hearts of the Atlantians melted and they withdrew. The fighting was over. The day had gone to the Athenians.

VIII

Althion arrived back at camp surrounded by a great host of men. He had stripped the polished armor from brave Alexius and had won great honor that day.

When he entered his tent, there sat Aerocles waiting to hear news of the battle.

"It seems you are victorious. Unless my eyes deceive me, you carry the armor of Prince Alexius."

"The day is ours my brother. I wish you had been there. Many heroic deeds are done today."

"Heroic deeds you say? I have killed more men than have died in all the wars of history. On the plane of Illustria I alone held the field against the Atlantian's. I alone fought against them in the Hill Country, in the forest, and on the open sea."

"Forgive me my champion, I did not mean to offend."

"No, it is I who am sorry. You are a faithful friend and brother. I will have my vengeance soon. Then it will be over."

IX

"My King" spoke the servant hesitantly.

"Who disturbs me?"

"My King, news of the battle has arrived"

"Very well" came the angry, half drunken voice.

The chamber was dark, though was midday. From the shadows, the sound of shuffling feet neared the door. The servant stepped aside as a young woman, wrapped only in a cloth, quickly fled and hurried down the stairs. She was extraordinarily beautiful with fair skin and long dark hair the trailed behind her. She was beautiful, or at least would have been if it were not for the shame upon her face and the tears that rolled down her cheeks. She was one of the kings many concubines, and one of his favorites. He heard her weeping as she descended the stairs.

"Spit it out man" said the King. "Have the Athenian dogs left our shores?"

"No sire" replied the servant. "They have won the day. And what is more, Prince Alexius has fallen at the hand of Althion."

"Alexius" the king muttered the name as if only half remembering. "Alexius. His mother was a whore if there ever was one. The world should of been rid of him long ago. Disturb me again only if something worthy occurs." He turned back towards his chamber, agitated and having gotten up for such petty matters.

"If I may sire, it has been three days since our naval reinforcement should have returned from their exploits in Corsica, yet there has been no word of their fate."

"Naval reinforcements? Ha! Atlantia will not fall today nor any other day. Naval reinforcements or not."

"But the men sire, they are wondering–"

"The men?!" shouted the King, suddenly angry. "The men should remember that they are here to serve me and me alone. It is my will that gives them life or takes it away. And you too should remember that." He paused. The anger that flashed across his face subsided. "Now, bring me meat and wine!"

At dawn the next day, the sun rose slowly over the battlefield where so many heroes had fallen the day before. As the life-giving sunlight descended upon the bronze and silver armies, there arose a shout from the Atlantian ranks. Theron, a noble captain and dear friend of brave Alexius, rose over the din as the Greeks approached.

"Noble brothers" he began. "Do not fear them. Do not fear their shields or their spears. Do not fear the blade of mighty Aerocles, for he is not among them. News has reached me that he will not be in the fighting neither today nor the morrow. Be courageous, and remember that they are only men. This day you will return them to the dust from whence they came!"

A mighty roar went up from them after he had spoken. Many an experienced warrior also breathed a hidden sigh of relief as they heard that Aerocles, the slayer of men, would not be in the fighting. Emboldened, they marched eagerly toward their enemy.

XI

The days fighting began with a mighty heft of a spear from bold Patrus. Long it sailed over the bloodstained ground before hitting its Mark and felling a young charioteer. The young man staggered and fell backwards, his soul flying toward Heaven even as his body fell heavily to the ground.

Undaunted, the Atlantians descended upon the Greeks was unexpected ferocity. Power and strength filled their limbs as they pushed onward remembering the words of their captain. Many brave Greeks died that day. Even fearless Althion was powerless to rally his men and prevent so many from falling in a foreign land so far from home.

Has the Atlantian's pushed on further and further from the wall their advantage waned. When the sun was high, noble Theron and courageous Helios met on the field of battle. Theron spilled a steady stream of blood from his left shoulder the ran down behind his shield. Helios too had been wounded by an arrow that had pierced his right thigh when he ventured too close to the Atlantian wall. The pain of it staggered him. From beneath his bronze helmet, decorated with a high plume and a long tail, the mark of a captain, Helios eyed his enemy.

"There has been much death today" he said heavily, breathing hard from the battle.

Theron peered out from beneath his own helmet. In the voice of his opponent, he felt his own weariness.

"Aye. Many have fallen" he replied.

Suddenly they both felt a tremor in the ground. Despite the battle, many men stopped and looked at the mountain with a fearful expression.

"Perhaps we should give this day to the gods" said Helios.

Theron paused. Stealing a glance around himself he beheld the fighting and slaughter. The Atlantians held the advantage, but his men were tiring. He took in a long breath and let it out slowly.

"There is only one God Athenian. But yes, let us give the rest of this joyless day to Him."

With a slow tilt of his helm, Helios acknowledged and they both stepped back. At a signal from Theron's hand, a loud trumpet blew and sounded across the plain. Helios too sent a signal, and soon the fighting stopped.
The day was over.

XII

Far away, Lionisius finished preparing the ship he and his daughter Lydia would use for their escape. It was a small ship, but fast. One of the last Atlantian skiffs, renowned for their speed across the high seas.

Unlike the crude Greek rowboats, the Atlantian ships had a deep keel and two tall sails that leaned deep with the wind. Nearly every other ship in Atlantia had either been destroyed by war or taken by those fortunate souls who left to escape the fate of their city. Lionisius looked on his little ship with sadness, yet also with approval. It would make the journey.

XIII

That evening, Althion led a small raiding party across the countryside to see what provisions they may scavenge. At nightfall, when they return, they brought with them and unexpected prize.

"Who is this man you bring with you?" asked Aerocles.

"He is advisor to the King" replied Althion. "In the morning, captains will learn from him the Council of our enemy."

They chained him securely to a post and left him in the care of hooded Aerocles.

They sat together in silence for a long time. Both listening to the sound of the ways along the shore. Finally, the captain spoke.

"What will become of me?" He asked wearily.

"Your old man, Atlantian. And the fighting is for the young. If you speak well tomorrow then you will have nothing to fear" replied Aerocles.

"But you are a warrior, are you not? Are you not here to kill?"

Aerocles pulled back his hood to reveal his face. "I am Aerocles, son of Perocles. I have killed more men than have been born in all of Athens." He paused. "Does that frighten you?"

"No. Death does not frighten a man as old as I. I fear only for my daughter. We were trying to flee this place for God has cursed it because of the evil our Kings have brought."

"The gods give no thought to man" replied Aerocles. "They smile and laugh as we fall and die and are no more."

"There is only one God Aerocles, and he thinks of you often. If one good thing survives the evil that has corrupted Atlantia, may it be the knowledge of our Father who has created us all."

"You are mistaken old man. If there was such a God he would have saved you from being a captive."

"Perhaps he has sent me here for a reason. Search your heart Aerocles, and know this, before this war is over you will be given a choice between life and death and you will know there is a God who sees you."

"I will make such an end to your people, that if there is a God, he would **have to** be blind to not see it."

"Mighty Aerocles, you have been given the power to end lives and have become familiar with death and grief. But of life and love, you have much to learn."

XIV

On the third day, the sun did not rise. Clouds start with sky and heavy rain fell upon the battlefield. The cries of men rang with the lightning and thunder and blood ran in thick streams between the fallen.

Fierce was the fighting that day. In the end, bold Patrus raised his sword against brave Theron and would have killed him, if not for an ill-fated arrow pierced his chest.

His men caught him before he fell to the ground and carried him from battle. They brought him to his tent where they were to care for him, but he would not have it.

"No" he said. "I want to feel the rain." He breathed heavily, his life ebbing away. They laid him out carefully under the stormy sky and he watch the clouds roll by a swift wind.

"Send for Aerocles" he said finally.

Word went out, and soon Aerocles arrived. He looked down at his captain, at the mortal wound in the blood that flowed into the sand. The end was near for him.

"Aerocles" he said weakly. Kneeling down, Aerocles leaned in and held his brother's hand. "I have been a fool Aerocles. I compared my strength to yours and in my pride thought I was the better man. But I see now, it is you who will lead these men to victory. It is you who will get them home." At this, Patrus lifted his ornate helmet and pushed it toward Aerocles.

"Forgive me, for I did not see. You are captain now. Do for them what I could not."

Aerocles, stricken with grief, felt the life leave his brother's hand. He knelt there, weeping in the rain, for a long time.

XV

Lionisius sat shivering in the rain. Thoughts of his daughter filled his mind and he worried for her. He wondered what would become of her. Gradually, he heard the sound of footsteps behind him. He had told the Athenians everything he knew of the Atlantian stratagem that morning and so his purpose had run its course. As the footsteps approached he heard the smooth metallic sound of a sword being drawn. He closed his eyes. Surely, this was the end. He could not fight or run for the chain that held him.

As the sword came down however, he felt the chain snap and fall away. There before him stood Aerocles.

"You are my messenger" he said. "Go back to your city and tell them there that before the sun is at its height tomorrow, all of Atlantia will be set aflame by my hand."

XVI

Lydia made her way back to her home. She had been searching for any sign of her father for hours but to no avail. Her heart trembled insider her at the thought of what may have become of him. As she rounded the corner of a stone pillar she stopped suddenly. In front of her was a hooded figure, a woman, with an incredibly sad countenance.

"Excuse me" said the woman. She spoke in a quiet voice, her eyes never leaving the ground. The woman moved to continue her slow, grievous walk, but something inside Lydia made her reach out to her.

"Wait" she said. "Who are you and why do you look so?"

"I am the Kings servant" she replied. "And even now he calls for me."

Lydia then recognized her cloak and dress is one of the Kings heroin. Even though Atlantia lake crumbling, he could think of nothing else. Her heart pitied the woman.

"You do not have to go" she said unexpectedly. The woman looked at her as if to speak but Lydia continued quickly. "My father has a ship. We leave tonight upon his return. Come with us. Let us leave this unhappy place and start anew in another land."

Tears welled up in the woman's eyes. "I cannot" she said finally. "I have tried escape. I have tried to flee but..." she trailed off and sadness. Then, composing herself, she straightened and wiped the tears from her eyes. What remained of her shattered nobility gradually returned. "I must go" she said. And with that she moved on.

Lydia watched as she walked slowly and mournfully away. Then, she suddenly stopped and let out a long breath. Lydia's heart rose at the thought that she may have reconsidered. The woman turned her head and spoke over her shoulder, her eyes hidden beneath the cloak.

"My name is Sola" she said. "Is it a fast ship?"

XVII

Lionisius return home. It was late in the evening and the house was empty. It had taken him a long time to slip through the secret passageways and back into the city without being noticed. He searched the house. It was dark. Lydia was gone. Then came a loud and heavy knock upon the door. Opening it, he found two soldiers with fierce appearance before him.

"Lionisius" began one of the soldiers. "Your daughter Lydia has been found trying to leave the city. She is accused of desertion during war and is being held in the palace dungeon."

"You fool. Atlantia has already fallen and you would keep those who would live from escaping." He paused, reining in his anger. "Take me to her."

*   *   *

"I am so sorry" said Lydia through the bars of her cell. Lionisius tried to contain himself as he watched her tears streamed down her face. "I thought you might have been captured or worse" she said. "When you did not return I feared the worst. I am so sorry. I even brought another with me, but they took her also, I know not where."

"No my daughter, it is I who am to blame. If I had not been so foolish as to let myself be caught by the Athenians I would have returned long before this could have happened."

"Is there no hope then? Is this how it is all to end?"

"No my dear. There must be a way. There must be someone..." he trailed off, thinking desperately.

"Perhaps the King will have mercy if you spoke to him" she said.

"There has not been mercy in Atlantia for a long time. No. I must speak with the Athenians."

XVIII

It was now nighttime. The rain in clouds had given way to a brilliant moon that shine down upon Aerocles as he sat along the shore looking out to the sea.

Life and love. These are the things Lionisius has said he had much to learn of. And he was right. He had only known war his entire life. There had been no time for love or mercy or kindness. There had only been the love for his brothers, his men, his fellow soldiers. His only constant companions had been his sword, his spear, and his shield. Would he ever know love before the end?

As he thought, he heard the sound of someone approaching. He turned, and there before him was Lionisius exhausted and out of breath.

"You are either very brave, or very foolish old man" he said. "Why have you come here again after I released you to your people?"

Lionisius gathered himself before speaking. "I come to you on the half the one I love. My daughter. She is being held in the palace dungeon for trying to escape."

"What business is that of mine?" Asked Aerocles.

Lionisius fell to his knees and looked up at him. "You are a great champion and captain of your people. Surely the Athenians will take the city tomorrow and you will have your victory. But I beg you, spare the life of my daughter. Have mercy upon her when your men enter the city."

Love. Mercy. Kindness. These words echoed in his soul like a distant cry caught in the wind. But something in his spirit stirred. That gears of his heart turned unexpectedly and he felt pity for this man. Suddenly, he was no longer just an Atlantian, but a father begging for the life of his daughter. He felt compassion for the first time and so long.

"Peace, old man. Peace. Your supplication has won me. I will see to it that no one harms you or your daughter. Tomorrow, be sure to hang a white cloth outside the passageway the dungeon and no Athenian will enter. Likewise, Thai white cloth around your right arm both you and your daughter, and you will be spared. Do it not, and you will be swept away with the rest."

XIX

All was dark and silent. It was a starless morning, long before dawn. There in the darkness, the shadowy man emerged from his tent. He carried a shield on his left arm, a sword upon his belt, and held a long spear, straight and true, and his right hand. Upon his head was the bronze helmet of a captain, a tall black plume a long tail of horsehair. His stature was fearsome to behold. Fear went out before him. Power and strength filled every step of his purposeful stride. Glory would be his this day.

Aerocles was ready for battle.

XX

Quintus and Helios also rose early. As the sun broke over the sea, there stood Aerocles upon an embankment shining in the first light of morning. They beheld his might and stature, looking like a god of war in the early breeze. His face was turned toward the city of his enemies as he waited for the others to assemble.

"He wears the helm of fallen Patrus" said Helios.

"Aye" replied wise Quintus. "The gods have ordained that he should lead us this day."

"Let us go up to him then, and counsel together."

Arriving beside him, the three commander spoke.

"Bold Patrus would be honored to have you command in his stead" said Quintus. "As well as I."

"And I" added Helios. After a moment he asked "what is your mind concerning the battle?"

"I have watched your battles these last few days" said Aerocles. "You are strong at the flanks, so I will take the center in place of our brother Patrus. I only ask that when the fighting starts, you grant the a wide birth. In the fury of the fighting I do not wish to mistake a friend from an enemy."

"It shall be done" replied Helio's. "And what of this family spoke of? If the city falls and we happen upon them, what shall we do?"

"The city will fall. When you find them, no harm shall come to them. Lead them away from the city and released them. These are my orders."

XXI

Theron watched as thick smoke poured from the mountain. Black clouds covered the southern sky and a dark shadow fell upon the city. He knew the end was near. If not by the Greeks, then by the mountain. The time of Atlantia was over.

He looked at the men about him.

"Sons of Atlantia" he began. "My brothers. My friends. On these last days you have fought with strength and honor. You have brought glory to our people. But I ask that you bleed with me one last time." He moved through the ranks grasping each man's shoulder and looking him straight in the eye.

"We will have victory over our enemies!" Victory in life! Victory in death! Victory in the sun and victory in the shadow! Let us make such an end to our enemies that all of Heaven will sing of this day for all time!

But be not deceived, there is no more refuge in the city. There is nowhere to flee, nowhere to hide." He donned his silver helmet then, its red and black plume the color of crimson. "Today will be our last battle, and if we die, we all die together."

A great shout rang out from the Atlantian ranks. So loud was their cry that it shook the ground and echoed out across the plain to the advancing Athenians.

Just then, before the Athenians could fully deploy, the Atlantians did the unthinkable. They charged from the safety of their walls with full force and fury. They had no strategy. No plan. All else had been exhausted. All that remained was strength and fury. Might and glory.

Like a wounded beast who knows the end is near, the poured themselves out upon their enemies, reserving nothing. For the Atlantians, there was no retreat, no falling back. No reserve to bring relief.

It was victory or death.

At the head of the charge was brave Theron, his armor blazing even in the shadow of the mountain. He fell upon the Athenians, slaughtering her sons without mercy. Many fell at his hand that day. Aerocles, some distance away, saw the glory of Theron. In his heart he smiled and thought *"perhaps today there will be a worthy fight indeed."*

The clash of battle rose up toward Heaven. As sword met shield, men fell in droves beneath a hail of spears. Angels and demons alike stopped and quaked at the maelstrom. The ground shook and the wind began to blow. Far away, great plumes of smoke poured from the mountain. Souls of the fallen flew off to either bliss or woe, and as they did, were caught up in its shadow like a rising funeral pyre. A sign of lament for a once just people.

Aerocles was circled 'round about by bodies, piled high in the fighting. Even so, the Atlantians advanced. They descended upon him with ferocity and passion, the likes of which he had never seen, and he gloried in it. His sword flashed like lighting. His every motion filled with purpose and death. Yet on they came.

As the fighting continued, Aerocles found himself alone. Looking 'round, he saw through the fierce fighting brave Theron afar off. His heart burned to fight him. This was the man who felled his captain. Not only this, but he was perhaps the last worthy enemy in all Atlantia. He moved toward him, but then beheld another thing.

Elsewhere, across the battlefield his men were scattered. The Athenian ranks had fallen into chaos amidst the fury of the enemy. Each man fought alone with no one beside him. His men were dying.

He looked back toward Theron, his heart full of bloodlust and rage. It was then the words of Lionisius echoed in his mind. This was the choice. To bring low brave Theron would win him glory beyond measure, but at the cost of his men who he was to lead.

He paused. He felt the breath in his powerful lungs. He felt the cold blood that covered his body and watched it fall like crimson rain from his sword. This was the choice. His own glory and vengeance, or the lives of his men.

He breathed, long and slow.

In the end, it was the love of his brothers that stayed him. He turned and fought his way back to the middle of the plain. Here, the fighting was most fierce. Regaining his spear, he came alongside a fellow Greek whose name he did not know, and braced his shield against his own. With a great shout, his voice rang over the thunder of battle.

"As one!" he cried.

Althion then joined him on his right, and then another Greek soldier and another. Soon, a line began to form, each man defending the other. The mighty push of the enemy began to slow. The Greeks held fast, strengthened by the might of their captain. First merely holding, then pushing forward. Aerocles thrust forward with a shout, and the wall of shields advanced, one step, and then another. Gradually, the tide of battle began to turn.

Theron felt the change and saw the Greeks regrouping. He rallied his men and charged the wall of bronze, but the strength of the Athenians would not be broken. His men were falling, His own brothers were dying. He looked for Aerocles.

*   *   *

When they met, they spoke no words. Aerocles stepped out from the wall of shields alone amidst his enemies. Theron and Aerocles circled each other like wolves. Aerocles struck first with a fierce thrust of his spear. Theron however, was swift and parried the blow with his shield, rending the flesh of Aerocles with his spear-point as his did so. Aerocles groaned with pain. *"Finally, a worthy enemy"* he thought.

They went back and forth, testing each other, trying to put the other off balance. Theron advanced again with a mighty thrust but the shield of Aerocles stayed the point and it became lodged. Aerocles hefted his own spear at Theron, narrowly missing him. He threw down his shield, now useless, and produced his blade. Theron saw this, and in a display of honor cast away his own shield. He stood before his enemy, sword in hand.

In his soul, Theron knew this would be his end. He had seen this moment before in his dreams. The time of his people was over. The walls that stood guard over his city for so long would fall. No longer would ships come into its harbor. No more would there be sounds of children laughing in its streets. No more would he see his loving wife or another sunrise.

Brave Theron summoned all his strength and swung at Aerocles. His enemy staggered back and Aerocles could feel the wind of his blade at his neck.

Then, Aerocles seized the moment. He quickly advanced, parried his enemy's blow with a turn and brought his own sward 'round behind him and thrust it into the chest of Theron. He turned again, and looked him in the eyes as he pushed his blade through to the hilt.

Theron gasped and felt his life ebb away. Looking at Aerocles, he saw in his eyes that if times were different they could have been friends. His soul was like his own. Then his eyes drifted up toward the mountain. Suddenly, as though it had been waiting for the last just man of Atlantia to fall, the mountain exploded.

His body fell heavily to the ground and the Earth quaked with his fall. With the death of Theron, the last true light of Atlantia burned out. Heaven's restraint was now removed and the wrath of God fell upon the city. A deafening roar was heard on the wind and with a great blast, the mountain blew apart. Immense boulders of flaming rock hurtled skyward. The city walls cracked and fell as they smashed into the stonework.

Every man, both Atlantian and Greek, trembled at the sight.

XXII

Down in the palace dungeon, Lionisius hugged his daughter through the iron bars of her cell. For hours, the sounds of war had been steadily approaching. Thunder raged outside. The building shook and dust rained down from the ceiling. Now they heard footsteps, running, and great commotion down the hall and shouts within the corridor.

"Do not be afraid my daughter. All will be well" he said.

Just then, the dungeon door flew open and the lifeless body of a guardsman fell heavily down the stairs. A black shadow filled the doorway, the silhouette of a man with drawn sword.

He stepped heavily down the stairs and over the body of the guardsman as if it were nothing. He looked down at the old man and his terrified daughter as they held each other. A white band of silk about each of their arms.

"Are you Lionisius?" he asked with a commanding voice.

"I am. And this is my daughter, Lydia."

"Do not fear me. I am Helios, friend of Aerocles. I am here to escort you out of the city. Move quickly, for we have little time."

XXIII

Aerocles, along with Althion and his men, stormed the palace sparing no one. Inside, they found a group of Atlantian nobles, a huddled group of fifty frightened men, cowering in the Great Hall. These same men were those who designed so much evil against the world. Cowards, each one. In their lives, they had shown no pity and therefore received none now. Aerocles and those with him drew their swords and slaughtered every one of them. None of them were brave enough to draw a sword or fight back even as they watched their own kinsmen fall. Their evil blood ran thick upon the floor. When it was over, Aerocles looked upon their bodies with disgust. Then moved on.

Outside, falling rock and debris continued to rain down upon the land like hail. Dust and ash also began to creep into the city. Earlier, when the city walls had been breached, wise Quintus had withdrawn from the fighting with his men and fell back to ready the ships. Aerocles was suddenly grateful he had done so, for he could just start to smell the ash as it came in through the windows. Soon, they must be away.

Finally, they came to the king's chamber. They encountered no resistance; the palace guards having fled their posts long ago. He wondered if the king himself remained.

A muffled noise from within answered his thoughts. The guards must have not spared a word to their king as they left, such was their loyalty. Inside, he had continued on with his lustful indulgences unaware of the coming calamity.

Aerocles nodded to his men and they took up positions around the heavy door. In a rage, he kicked it in, its latch and hinges splintering like straw. He stepped in.

Inside, he found the Atlantian king, covered in sweat and reeking of body odor and wine. His royal tunic hung loosely from his shoulders as though he had not changed in days. Upon his face was shock and sudden fear as he sprang from his bed and pressed against the wall.

Aerocles scorned with disgust. He would have killed him right then and there, but as he stepped forward, another thing stole his attention.

There at his feet he found a slave girl, a woman, huddled on the floor against the wall. She would not so much as look up at him, but kept her face downcast to the floor accepting her fate. Aerocles had seen death countless times in countless battles, yet here was a woman who looked as though she had died a thousand times, and now welcomed the end. He looked back at the cowardly king and guessed at her misery.

He brought up his sword, turned it around, and lifted her face with its pommel. Their eyes met, and in the light of her face he saw a beauty and tenderness he had never known before. It angered him that such a one was subjected to this torture. For the longest time, he had imagined felling the king of his great enemy but now, he knew that honor belonged to another.

"Take it" he said finally.

Her eyes blazed to life. She took the heavy sword in her hands, its weight being no match for her rage, and turned in fury toward her capture. Aerocles stepped out of the room.

A moment later, he heard a pitiful plea for help, then a loud scream like that of a child, a crash, and then silence.

Aerocles gave her another moment, then returned. Inside, blood was everywhere. It stained the walls, the ceiling, the carefully knit tapestries. There upon the bed lay the slaughtered king, the woman's sword buried to the hilt through his chest. He watched as she wrenched it from his lifeless body.

She backed away, blood streaming down her delicate face and form, and strode toward him with a cool, stately stride. Confidence and nobility returned to her once lifeless face.

"It is over" she said.

"…Aye. It is over" he replied quietly.

He gathered his men, and together they fled the crumbling palace.

XXIV

They made their way back to the proud Athenian ships along the shore. After setting off, Aerocles stood and looked on as smoke and thick darkness enveloped what remained of the once great city. Soon, he was joined by Aurora who stood beside him. Together, they watched the city of Atlantia disappear.

Far away, another ship tilted in the evening breeze, gliding effortlessly across the waves. It was an Atlantian ship, yet it bore the standard of Athens and the mark of Helios. At the stern stood an old man and beside him a young girl. They waved at him from across the distance.

Just then, he felt a warm hand slip into his and he looked down. Looking up at him were the fiery eyes of Aurora. His heart melted. Here before him was mercy he did not deserve. Here was kindness and gentleness. Here was love. This, he suddenly realized, was true glory.